W9-BNO-166

SECRET STUFF

Comic books

rock Collection

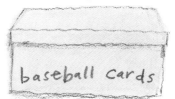
baseball cards

MORE TOP
SECRET
stuff

For Elizabeth and Nora:
may you always like where you are.
—J.H.

For Dawson, Jolie, and Wally.
—G.B.K.

Text copyright © 2004 by Jessica Harper. Illustrations copyright © 2004 by
G. Brian Karas. All rights reserved. This book, or parts thereof, may not be
reproduced in any form without permission in writing from the publisher,
G. P. Putnam's Sons, a division of Penguin Young Readers Group, 345 Hudson Street,
New York, NY 10014. G. P. Putnam's Sons, Reg. U.S. Pat. & Tm. Off. The scanning,
uploading, and distribution of this book via the Internet or via any other means
without the permission of the publisher is illegal and punishable by law. Please
purchase only authorized electronic editions, and do not participate in or
encourage electronic piracy of copyrighted materials. Your support of the author's
rights is appreciated. Published simultaneously in Canada. Manufactured in China
by South China Printing Co. Ltd. Designed by Gina DiMassi. Text set in Jacoby Light.
Library of Congress Cataloging-in-Publication Data  Harper, Jessica. I like where I am /
Jessica Harper ; illustrated by G. Brian Karas.  p. cm.  Summary: The rhyming story
of a six-year-old boy who is sad about moving to a new home but ends up being
happy when he gets there.  [1. Moving, Household—Fiction. 2. Stories in rhyme.]
I. Karas, G. Brian, ill. II. Title. PZ8.3.H219 Ih 2004 [E]—dc21 2001019922
ISBN 0-399-23479-9    10 9 8 7 6 5 4 3 2 1    First Impression

# I Like Where I Am

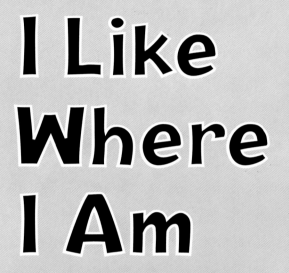

Jessica Harper

illustrated by **G. Brian Karas**

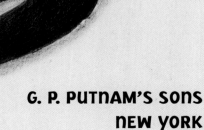

G. P. PUTNAM'S SONS
NEW YORK

I've got Trouble......
    I've got
        BIG TROUBLE......

'Cause I'm sittin' in my house
        on Willow Street
And I love this house.
        I love this street.
A prettier house
        you'll never meet
And I like where I am.
Yes, I like where I am.

That's why I've got Trouble.

'Cause I'm just kinda, you know, sittin',
Just messin' around with Mimi's kitten.
That's Mimi over there,
        in the little red chair.
She's usually got food in her hair.
She's not even two,
        so it's really not fair
That she's got a kitten
        and  I don't.

And I'm six.

Well, anyway . . .
I'm sittin' with a kitten
     and a piece of string,
Just listening to my mama sing:

"La la, la la, la la!"

And I like where I am.

toys

baby things

linens

I'm sittin' around and a truck shows up
And it's all bright red, this giant truck,
With two big men,
        they're REALLY big men!
Eight feet tall, or nine or ten!
They say,

    "Hi, son, can we come in, please?"

Two men, as big and strong as trees....
They make me feel all wobbly-knees!
They say,
        "HI, SON!"
                and that means me,
And that means I've got Trouble....

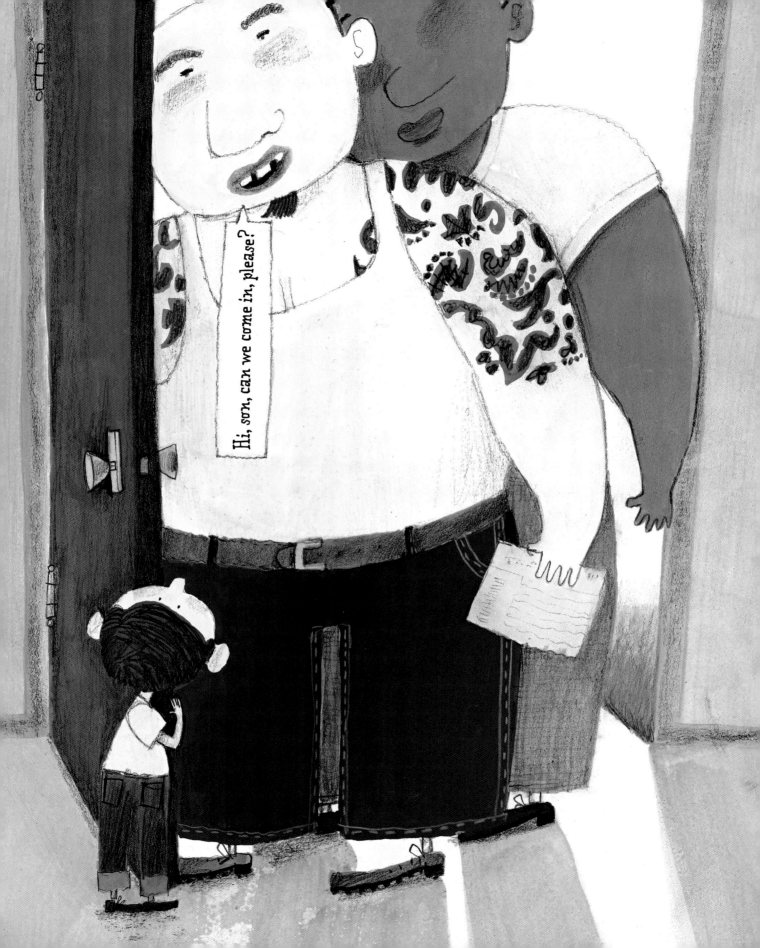

They say, "Hey, son, it's moving day!"
That's right, it's moving day.
They're gonna pick us up and take us away.
And I think (but I'm too scared to say),
Oh, why don't you just go away!
Take your truck and take your Trouble and
Move somebody else!

'Cause I like my room and I like my school,
And we live real close to a swimming pool,
And my best friend lives around the block.
Why move to a place called Little Rock
Anyway?

The two big men kinda chuckle at me,
With a ho ho ho and a hee hee hee.
My mama takes me on her knee
And sings a gentle song to me.
She rocks me back and forth.

"La la, la la, la la."

We watch the men walk back and forth
With a ho ho ho and a hee hee hee.
My tears drop down on Mama's knee.

shiny rocks
lava rocks
big rocks
tipping rocks
gold rocks

Books

They pack all our stuff in their truck—
There goes Mimi's rubber duck!
They take my bike and then my mama's.
Look! They've got my dad's pajamas!

"Everything goes!"
they say with glee,
With a ho ho ho and a hee hee hee,
And I know I've got Trouble!

'Cause I like my room and I like my school.
We live real close to a swimming pool
And my best friend lives around the block.
Why move to a place called Little Rock
Anyway?

But we did . . . . . . just like that.

And guess what?

Do you know what?

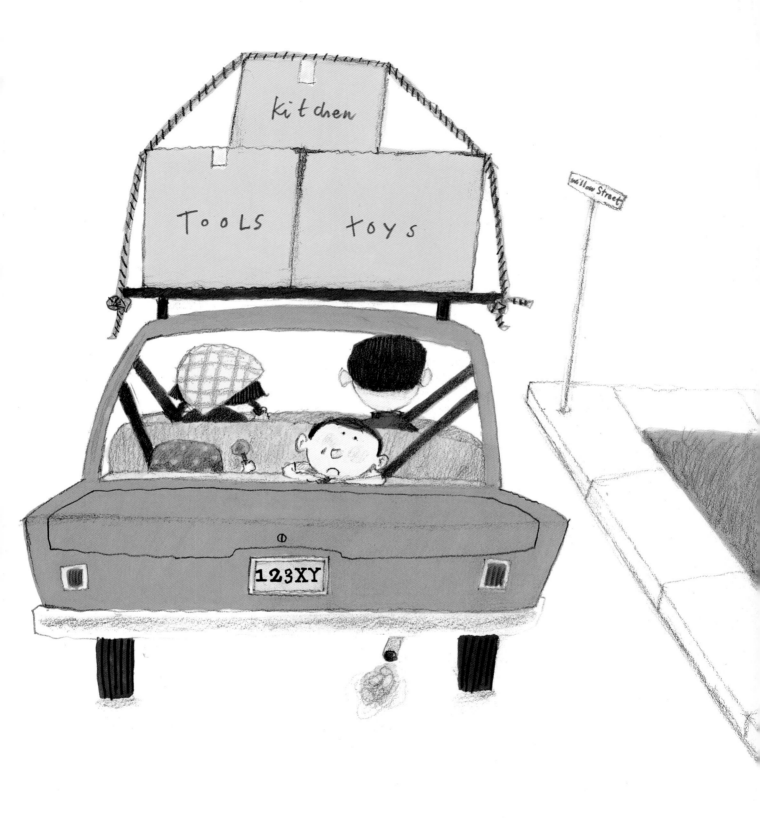

We moved to a place called Little Rock
And my new friend lives
        just up the block!
He even has a swimming pool.
My room's okay and so's my school. . . .
And I've got my own kitten!

I still think of Willow Street.
The memory is very sweet.
I'll always love where I was born . . .
But when I wake up in the morning,
I like where I am!

With a ho ho ho and a hee hee hee.
I like where I am!